For Susan Bergholz
My Warrior Mama—Tita out. Ack up always.
—L.-A.Y.

This is for all of the kids of color growing up in Hawai'i, who dream of a world
that diverges from the legacy of colonization and militarization—
a different Hawai'i is possible. Thank you to the Kanaka Maoli for teaching us
about your land and how vital it is to protect it—Ku Kia'i Mauna.
—A.L.

I lift up the depth and breadth of my gratitude to you:

JohnJohn Inferrera, Nohea Kanaka'ole, Harry Yamanaka, Carla Yamanaka, Charles
Tatsuhara, Aunty Gladys Yoon, Laura Lee Kawabata, Gary Yamanaka; Michelle Frey,
Chris Myers, Jennifer Lyons, Lori Carlson; Claire-Bear Shimizu, Don Sumada, Teddy Cancilla;
R. Zamora Linmark, Nora Okja Keller, Tae Keller, mi amada Sandra Cisneros, Lisa Asagi,
Morgan Blair, Wing Tek Lum; Na'au Learning Center 'Ohana, treasured students, and
families; Keli'i Ruth, Mel and Keoki; Suzette and Junette Shigemasa, Mommy and Pops
and the best Hilo Lunch Shop warabi; Louella, Glenn, Martin, Jyric, and Doreen Ellazar;
Beautiful Boyd, Gayle Kutaka, Makala Cooke; Lynette Romero, Glenn Nakaya, Janis Otake,
Malie Chong, Falakai, Junko, and Iva; and Timbo—my Patrick "Straight-Outta-Puna."
For all of you, I praise and thank God, from whom all blessings flow, for always.
MAHALO!
Lois

MAKE ME A WORLD is an imprint dedicated to exploring the vast possibilities of contemporary childhood. We strive to imagine a universe in which no young person is invisible, in which no kid's story is erased, in which no glass ceiling presses down on the dreams of a child. Then we publish books for that world, where kids ask hard questions and we struggle with them together, where dreams stretch from eons ago into the future and we do our best to provide road maps to where these young folks want to be. We make books where the children of today can see themselves and each other. When presented with fences, with borders, with limits, with all the kinds of chains that hobble imaginations and hearts, we proudly say—no.

Text copyright © 2021 by Lois-Ann Yamanaka
Jacket art and interior illustrations copyright © 2021 by Ashley Lukashevsky

All rights reserved. Published in the United States by Make Me a World,
an imprint of Random House Children's Books, a division of Penguin Random House LLC, New York.

Make Me a World and the colophon are registered trademarks of Penguin Random House LLC.

Visit us on the Web! rhcbooks.com

Educators and librarians, for a variety of teaching tools, visit us at RHTeachersLibrarians.com

Library of Congress Cataloging-in-Publication Data is available upon request.
ISBN 978-0-593-12737-7 (trade) — ISBN 978-0-593-12738-4 (lib. bdg.) — ISBN 978-0-593-12739-1 (ebook)

The text of this book is set in 13-point Filson Pro.
The illustrations were created using an iPad Pro with Procreate.
Book design by Nicole de las Heras
MANUFACTURED IN CHINA
October 2021
10 9 8 7 6 5 4 3 2 1
First Edition

Random House Children's Books supports
the First Amendment and celebrates the right to read.

SNOW ANGEL,
SAND ANGEL

WRITTEN BY

LOIS-ANN YAMANAKA

ILLUSTRATED BY

ASHLEY LUKASHEVSKY

MAKE ME A WORLD

New York

Mrs. Kurokawa is teaching us about seasons: autumn, winter, spring, and summer. The whole class will make dioramas about the season they pick out of her straw beach hat.

"Don't let me get winter," I say to myself. I reach in and spin the little papers around:

Winter.

I've never even *seen* real snow!

My brother, Timbo, gets winter, too. To decorate his diorama, he uses cotton balls for snow on the ground. Dried branches for dormant trees. And white glitter to sprinkle on cotton-ball bald spots. He *even* makes little origami snowflakes that hang from fishing line over his snowman.

My father helps me finish mine. "Migration," I write.

"Some birds fly away because it gets too cold." And then I stop.
"The birds don't fly *away* from Hawai'i in the winter. They come home."

"You're right, Claire-Bear," my father says. "In the wintertime, the
golden plover comes home to our backyard. He's skinny and hungry
from flying three thousand miles nonstop from Alaska!"

I put my golden plover in the middle of the field.

But this all makes me sad. I have never seen snow.
"We have snow here in Hawai'i," my father tells me. "I'll drive you to
Mauna Kea after the next storm." My eyes grow big with excitement.

And that very weekend, he takes my mother, Timbo, and me to the top of the tallest mountain in the world, if you measure from seafloor to summit.

But the snow on Mauna Kea isn't anything like I imagined.

"Why is this snow like blocks from the Hilo Ice Factory?"

"It's three days old," my father sighs. "We're too late for the fine snow. The storm came on Wednesday night."

"Old snow," I mutter.

Someday, I will live in a place with new snow, not the old snow like we have on Mauna Kea, Big Island of Hawai'i.

"Don't run around too much on the summit or you'll get dizzy," my father reminds me. "We're nearly inside the heavens. There's a lot less oxygen up here, so you better take it easy."

"Oh, cripes," I tell him, out of breath, and so dizzy I think I'll be sick. "They run around in snow in the movies."

Someday, I will open my back door, run through a yard piled high with white snow, and never get altitude sickness. We won't have to drive miles and miles up a winding road between gray and black lava fields, fallen 'ōhi'a lehua trees, and patches of scrub grass just to get to the snow.

"Protect your hands, so you don't get frostbite. And don't aim snowballs at Timbo's head," my father chides.

"Some mittens," I grumble,

"and some snowballs."

Someday, I won't have to wear my father's old socks, loose and wet, over my cold hands. I will put on real mittens, and I'll make soft, fluffy snowballs, not the crunchy, icy wads that nearly knock Timbo over.

"Sorry, Claire, but you have to keep warm," my mother says as she pulls a beanie tight over my ears. "This is all we've got."

Someday, I will have a real snow hat. And a real wool scarf, not an old beach towel that my mother cuts in half for Timbo and me to wear around our necks.

"Cheer up!" my mother calls to us as she tries to snap some pictures. "No way!" I yell back. I glare at the camera while Timbo herky-jerks me on the sugarcane truck inner tube between the sharp points of rocks. Someday, I will ride a real sled that whizzes smoothly over the snow.

Timbo makes two chunky mounds into a triangle-shaped body and head for our snowman. "I've got two tiny lava rocks for the eyes," he says, placing them in the melting mound.

"And I found this māmane branch for his pipe," my father says.

My mother puts an ume where his nose would be. "I made this pickled plum from our own tree."

They stand back and admire the lumps of ice.

"C'mon, Claire-Bear," my father calls. He places his ugly hunting cap on the stunted lump. Someday, I will make a real snowman straight from the books my father reads to me. I will roll snow around the yard until I make three huge balls for a giant snowman, with a corncob pipe and two eyes made out of coal, just like the song says.

Someday, I will see snow falling from the
sky and be like the Inuit, who can name a
hundred different kinds of snow.

"Native Hawaiians know the names of a hundred winds and all of the oceans' currents," my father tells me. "The stars, too. Each and every beautiful star."

I don't say anything. I'm thinking that I will become a *real* snow angel. I will grow wings and fly away, rise up from the highest mountain and take myself to another place, more beautiful and special than this island, the only place my father and *his* father before him have ever known. The only place I know.

My father takes us to Hapuna Beach the day before the New Year. "The beach is always right in your backyard," he says to me as he opens the car door to the smell of kiawe trees and ocean mist. I run over the sand, Timbo behind me, to the waters of Kawaihae, the same color of the cloudless sky over Mauna Kea. I make a sand ball and throw it at Timbo, who dodges it by slipping under a large winter swell.

"You've just given me an idea, Claire-Bear," my father says. He starts with his own ball of wet sand. He covers this with fine, dry sand, then wet sand again, then dry sand. Soon he has built a huge sandman.

"Use the two cowrie shells for his eyes," Timbo says, placing them in the sandman's head.

"And here's some driftwood for his pipe." My father hands a gray branch to Timbo. "A smooth pebble for his nose," offers my mother.

I begin gathering tiny pieces of white honeycomb coral. "For the sandman's smile," I tell them.

My mother finds seaweed for his long hair of many colors. Timbo wraps a beach-towel scarf around his neck. And my father places his own straw hat on the sandman's head.

I drag the sugarcane truck inner tube to the water. My poi dog, Spam, barks as my mother carries her surfboard into the first small wave. Then Spam and my mother hop on board.

My mother tells us the names of the sea creatures. Hinalea, beautiful green wrasse. Manini, striped convict tang. Lauhau, golden butterflyfish. Humuhumunukunukuāpua'a, painted triggerfish. She shows us the rise and fall of honu's tiny head and the glide of his shiny turtle shell.

My father names the hundred winds that carry the fragrance of these waters to us near the far reef.

I run up and down the sloping shore, the waves catching me only when I get tired. At the beach, I never feel dizzy or out of breath. "Come, Claire," my father says, calling me over. "Watch." Soon he is making a sand angel just for me. I lie down next to him.

Father angel. Mother angel. Son angel. Daughter angel. "You can grow wings in this place," he says, "this very beautiful place that we know so well."

I stand back and look at the magnificent sandman, the sand angels with wings that can fly over the mountains and waters of this island, singing the names of a hundred winds.

The tide begins to rise, filling sand angel wings with soft sea foam. I watch my sandman melt away. But I am not sad.

The setting sun is a volcanic orange sphere hovering above the horizon. A green flash of light follows it, that flash you see but once in a lifetime when the sun disappears on this beautiful island of lava fields, sandy beaches, rain forests, fiery volcanoes, sacred mountains, and, yes, even snow.

AUTHOR'S NOTE

My home, the Big Island of Hawai'i, contains ten of the *world's* fourteen climate zones. Climate zones are the weather patterns and temperatures of an area. From the time I was a little girl, I learned so much about endangered plants and animals, all living things, and life-giving materials like water, dirt, stones, and sand found nowhere else in the world. Even more amazing, in just ten miles of highway through the Hawai'i Volcanoes National Park, I experienced the wonders of seven of Hawai'i's ten climate zones! From beaches and lowland, midland, and upland rain forests to frosty, dry mountain slopes, and even snow-capped mountains, I treasured each as a gift.

Sometimes we think we are more powerful than the plants, insects, animals, rivers, rocks, sand, moss, and trees that have been here for millions of years, but really, we are all equal in the eyes of God. Sadly, climate change now damages *all living things* in Hawai'i. In fact, scientists call my home the Endangered Species Capital of the World. Many ocean, land, and sky creatures found only in Hawai'i fight for their survival.

However, scientists believe Mauna Kea is the best place on earth to build a Thirty Meter Telescope (TMT) as high as an eighteen-story building! It will allow scientists from many nations to study the evolution of our universe and even explore thousands of galaxies beyond our own.

The kia'i—or protectors of Mauna Kea—do not see this as a conflict between cultural traditions and scientific progress. The kia'i want to do what is right for Mother Earth—to protect her and honor her. Many indigenous peoples, like our kia'i, struggle for rights to safeguard their sacred lands.

My hope remains for you to respect and take care of the sacred living and life-giving gifts where you live. Then you, like me, can tell your children, and their children, about your courage in protecting the place you called home.

GLOSSARY

hinalea (hee-nuh-LEH-uh): an abundant reef fish that can change gender and color patterns during its life (but tastes yucky).

humuhumunukunukuāpua'a (hoo-moo-hoo-moo-noo-koo-noo-koo-ah-poo-AH-ah): a reef triggerfish and the official state fish of Hawai'i. (Now say *that* ten times fast!)

Kawaihae (kuh-WHI-hi): a harbor town on the west side of the island of Hawai'i that is rich in Hawaiian history. (Too rich for me to count the ways here.)

kōlea (KOH-leh-uh): the Pacific golden plover, which flies from Alaska to the Hawaiian Islands, covering nearly 3,000 miles in a single nonstop trip. Native Hawaiians believed the kōlea was a messenger of the gods. (One lived in my front yard and came back every year!)

lauhau (LOW [rhymes with *wow*]-how): a rare blue-striped butterflyfish found only in the Hawaiian Islands. Lauhau live in shallow reef waters near rocky shores. (They are beautiful but don't taste great.)

manini (mah-NEE-nee): a small reef fish, also called the convict tang because of its black and white stripes, which look like a prisoner's uniform. (They are delicious when deep-fried. We eat them, bones and all.)

Mauna Kea (MOW [rhymes with *wow*]-nuh KAY-uh): a mountain sacred to native Hawaiians, where many of their gods and goddesses live.

ʻōhiʻa lehua (oh-HEE-uh LEH-hoo-uh): trees, found *only* in Hawaiʻi, that belong to Pele, the volcano goddess. The lehua flower is the official flower of the Big Island, and according to Hawaiian legend, picking a lehua flower can cause it to rain. (I picked the lehua, and when it rained, my family blamed me.)

MAKE ME A WORLD

Dear Reader,

I'm from New York City. My mom and dad are from New York. We are New York people. When I first met people who weren't from New York, to tell the truth, I didn't believe them. When they told me that all the stores closed in their neighborhood around eight p.m., I wondered how they went shopping. When they said they had never had Ethiopian food, I wondered why they had never gone to an Ethiopian restaurant. When they said they couldn't wait to see the museums in New York, I wondered if they just didn't like the museums where they were from, and fell on the floor when some of them said that there weren't any museums in their hometown. It took me a while to realize that the things I saw as the basics of my existence—twenty-four-hour bodegas, basketball courts in every playground, and the Metropolitan Museum of Art—just didn't exist in these other places.

I imagined these strange other places, without music dripping from the cars, where you only heard one language as you walked through the town, exotic other worlds with names like Switzerland or Nebraska.

Snow Angel, Sand Angel is a book about different worlds, and how we imagine each other. In recent times, as has always been the case, the ability to imagine each other, to imagine the fullness, richness, and truth of another life, is ever more necessary and rare. In the able hands of a giant of literature from Hawaiʻi, Lois-Ann Yamanaka, and a soon-to-be giant, Ashley Lukashevsky, *Snow Angel, Sand Angel* is about the act of imagining other people's worlds, and how we can make those worlds our own—and seeing how much like home a faraway place can be.

Christopher Myers

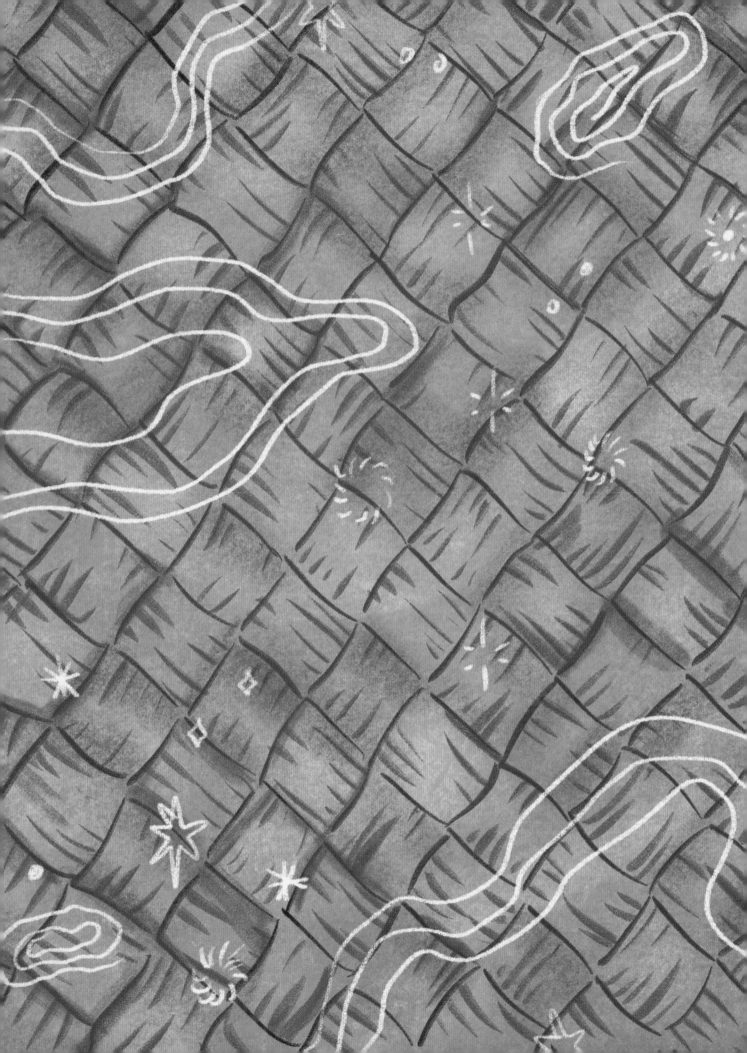